Seven Clues

A Catholic Treasure Hunt

Scott Hahn & Maura Roan McKeegan

Illustrated by Mercè Tous

LoyolaPress.
A JESUIT MINISTRY
Chicago

"And I saw...a scroll written within and on the back, sealed with seven seals..."

(Rev 5:1)

One Saturday morning, Peter and Julia were eating breakfast when they heard a knock at the front door.

"Who could that be?" asked Peter.

The children jumped up and ran to the front hallway.

Peter swung open the door and stared out into the morning air.

"No one's there," he said as Julia came up behind him.

"Look!" exclaimed Julia, pointing toward the ground. On the doorstep lay a box with a card attached to the top.

Peter leaned down to get a closer look.

"Who's it from?" asked Julia.

"I don't know. It doesn't say." Peter picked up the box, carried it to the kitchen table, and opened the card.

Here is what it said:

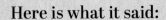

You're Invited

TO: An Eternal Banquet

DATE: The Day of the Sun

PLACE: Where Heaven Touches Earth
Follow the seven clues on the scroll
to find out more!

"Scroll? Seven clues?" Peter turned the card over, but nothing more was written on it.

Julia leaned over his shoulder and squinted at the invitation. "A banquet! Isn't that a big, fancy dinner with lots of people there?"

"Yes," replied Peter, "but...what does the rest of this mean? *The day of the sun? Where heaven touches earth?*"

Julia shook her head. "I have no idea."

Peter looked at the box sitting on the table. "Maybe we should open this."

The children opened the lid.

"This must be the scroll!" Julia reached inside, took out the rolled paper, and unfastened the ribbon. The curled paper was covered with writing. "And here are the seven clues!"

The children looked at the scroll.

"Now what do we do?" asked Julia.

"Well, it seems like a puzzle," said Peter. "And do you know who's good at solving puzzles?"

Just then, a teenager walked into the kitchen, wearing a bathrobe and slippers, and yawning.

Julia and Peter looked at each other and grinned.

"James!" Peter said. "Just the person we need. You're great at puzzles, and we could use your help with this one."

James rubbed his eyes. "What kind of a puzzle?" he asked sleepily.

"Sorry, James, I know you're half asleep, but this invitation just came, and we need you to help us figure out the clues." Peter showed the card and the scroll to James, who sat down to look at them more closely.

"Well," said James, beginning to wake up now, "when I want to solve a puzzle, I start at the beginning. Let's go through the clues one by one and see what we can figure out."

He pointed to the first lines on the scroll.

Clue #1: The banquet will begin with a sign.

(Hint: It is a sign that you make when you use your right hand to touch your forehead, then your heart, then your left shoulder, then your right.)

Reading the hint, Julia put her hand to her forehead, her heart, her left shoulder, and her right.

"It's the Sign of the Cross!" she cried.

"First clue solved!" Peter raised a victory fist in the air.

"Nice work," said James. "So, now we know that the banquet will begin with the Sign of the Cross. Let's take a look at the second clue."

Clue #2: A man in a long robe will be at a cloth-covered table.

(Hint: This robe is also called a vestment.)

Peter and Julia looked at James, sitting at the kitchen table in his long bathrobe.

"Don't look at me!" James put his hands up in the air. "I'm not going to a banquet in this! Anyway, my bathrobe is not called a vestment. But I know someone who does wear vestments."

"Who?" Peter and Julia asked at once.

"Over here." James pointed to a picture hanging in the hallway. It was of Peter on his First Communion Day. He was standing beside a man wearing a long robe.

"Father Paul!" Peter exclaimed. Their beloved pastor had taught them all about the different colored vestments he wore.

"If Father Paul will be there, I definitely want to go," said Julia. Father Paul was always making the children laugh with his antics and jokes. "I hope this means he'll be at our table."

"Maybe, but it also might not be Father Paul," said James. "All priests wear vestments, so it could be another priest, too."

"Either way," said Peter, "we can't go until we find out where and when it's happening. What does the third clue say?"

Clue #3: The people at the banquet will admit they've done wrong and ask for mercy.

(Hint: They will ask this from someone who has no beginning and no end.)

"Wait," said Peter. "What did they all do wrong?"

"I don't know," said James. "I think we should look carefully at the hint. Who are the people talking to? Who is someone with no beginning and no end?"

Peter bit his lip. "Um...I'm not sure."

"Think about it," said James. "Someone with no beginning and no end would have existed forever. Who has existed forever?"

"Oh!" exclaimed Julia. "Is it God?"

James gave her a high five. "You've got it!"

"So, the people at the banquet will ask for mercy from...God!" said Julia.

"But why?" asked Peter. "We still don't know what they did wrong. Are they all criminals? Is the banquet at a jail?"

"Not necessarily," replied James. "I mean, we're all guilty of doing wrong things sometimes, you know?"

"Yeah..." Peter looked guilty. He walked outside and pulled a basketball from the bushes. "I borrowed this yesterday without asking you," he said, handing the ball to James. "Sorry."

"I forgive you," said James, giving his brother a fist bump. "See? These people at the banquet are probably just like us. We all need God's mercy."

"OK," said Peter, "so the first three clues tell us that the banquet will start with the Sign of the Cross, that a priest will be at a table there, and that the people there will ask God for mercy. Now—on to clue number four."

Clue #4: You will hear a Word both Old and New.
(Hint: The Word is in a book that comes from God.)

"A word...that is old and new at the same time?" said Julia. "That doesn't make sense to me."

"It sounds complicated, but it might be simpler than you think," said James. "Can you think of a book that comes from God, like the hint says?"

"The Bible?" answered Julia.

"That's it!" Peter said, snapping his fingers. "The Bible has an Old and New Testament!"

"Good thinking!" said James. "And the Bible is the Word of God. So, that means, at the banquet, we will hear the Word of God from the Old and New Testaments of the Bible."

"We're more than halfway there!" Peter said. "What's the fifth clue?"

BIBLE

15

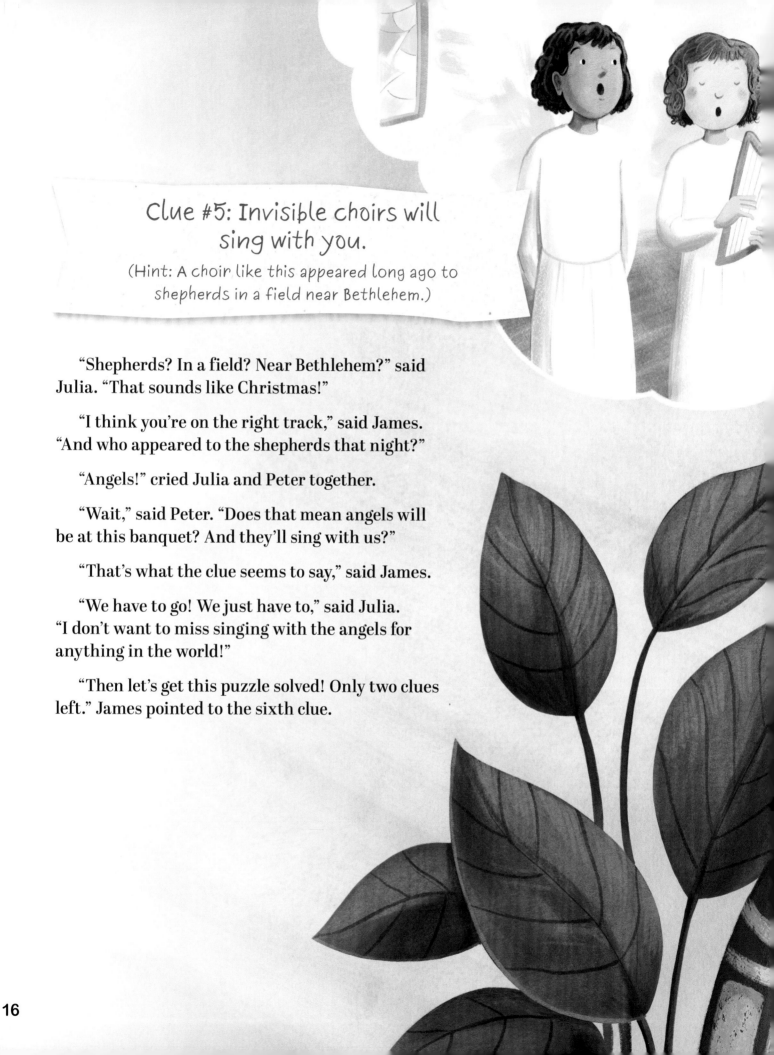

Clue #5: Invisible choirs will sing with you.
(Hint: A choir like this appeared long ago to shepherds in a field near Bethlehem.)

"Shepherds? In a field? Near Bethlehem?" said Julia. "That sounds like Christmas!"

"I think you're on the right track," said James. "And who appeared to the shepherds that night?"

"Angels!" cried Julia and Peter together.

"Wait," said Peter. "Does that mean angels will be at this banquet? And they'll sing with us?"

"That's what the clue seems to say," said James.

"We have to go! We just have to," said Julia. "I don't want to miss singing with the angels for anything in the world!"

"Then let's get this puzzle solved! Only two clues left." James pointed to the sixth clue.

Clue #6: A Lamb will be there.

(Hint: This Lamb gave His life as a sacrifice to save His people.)

"I'm lost," said Peter, shaking his head.

James laughed. "Wait here." He went upstairs, changed clothes, and came back down. "Let's go."

"Go? Where?"

"You'll see."

They walked two blocks and came to a place they all knew.

James rang the doorbell to the rectory, and a smiling priest answered.

The children smiled back. "Hi, Father Paul!" they said.

"Hey," Father Paul said, "I was just talking to my boss about you three!"

"Your boss?" Peter asked.

"Yeah, the best boss ever!" replied Father Paul. "Jesus is my boss. And this morning I was asking Him to bless you. What can I do for you?"

"Well," began James, "we have a question for you. We're trying to solve a puzzle, and we were wondering if you know anything about a lamb who sacrificed his life to save people?"

"A lamb? I sure do," said Father. "Have you ever heard the words, *Lamb of God, you take away the sins of the world?*"

"Oh, yes," said Peter. "At Mass!"

"Right, Peter!" said Father. "And do you know who the Lamb of God is?"

"Jesus?" replied Peter.

"Exactly," said Father. "You see, before Jesus was born, God saved the people of Israel from death by telling them to sacrifice a lamb. And then, Jesus came to earth to be that lamb—the Lamb of God, who would be sacrificed to save God's people."

"That helps a lot. Thanks, Father!" said Julia.

"Anytime," said Father Paul. "That's what I'm here for."

RITA'S CATHOLIC
CHURCH

After the children returned home, they looked at the scroll again.

"So," said Peter, "if the answer to that last clue is the Lamb of God... then Jesus will be at this banquet? How can that be true?"

"Maybe the last clue will tell us," said Julia.

Clue #7: You will share a meal both hidden and seen.

(Hint: To your eyes it looks like bread and wine, but truly
it's a Person who gives eternal life.)

"How can a meal be both hidden and seen?" Peter asked. "And doesn't a banquet usually have more for supper than bread and wine?"

"But remember, the hint says it only looks like bread and wine," James said. "And look at the rest! What looks like bread and wine, but is really a Person who gives eternal life?"

"I know!" Julia exclaimed. "The Eucharist!"

"That must be it," agreed Peter. "It looks like bread and wine, and that's the part of the meal that is seen. But it's really Jesus, and that's the hidden part."

"That means we figured out the answers to all the clues!" Julia clapped her hands. "Let's put them all together."

The children got a pencil and paper and made their own list.

Here is what it said:

Answers to the Clues

1. The banquet will begin with the Sign of the Cross.

2. A priest will be there at a cloth-covered table.

3. The people there will ask God for mercy.

4. We will hear something from the Old and New Testaments of the Bible.

5. An invisible choir of angels will sing with us.

6. The Lamb of God, Jesus, will be there.

7. The meal will be the Eucharist.

"Wait," said Peter, "that sounds like..."

"Mass!" Julia shouted. "The eternal banquet sounds just like Mass!"

Peter pointed to the second clue. "And the cloth-covered table is...the altar! It all makes sense now."

Julia picked up the invitation, and the children read it once more.

You're Invited

TO: An Eternal Banquet

DATE: The Day of the Sun

PLACE: Where Heaven Touches Earth
Follow the seven clues on the scroll to find out more!

"The day of the sun!" cried Peter. "That must be Sunday!"

"I think you're right," said James, nodding his head.

"But what about this part?" asked Julia. "*Where heaven touches earth?*"

Just then, there was another knock at the door. Peter and Julia looked at one another and ran to open it. This time, someone was there.

"Nana! Papa!" The children hugged their grandparents. "What are you doing here?"

"Well," said their grandfather with a twinkle in his eye, "we thought you probably would have solved the puzzle by now, and we came to make a confession."

"Confession? Aren't we supposed to go to Father Paul for that?" Julia asked.

"Normally, yes!" answered Papa. "But today, we have a confession to make to you. We know who knocked on your door this morning and left something for you on the doorstep. It was your grandmother and I."

"You?" The children stared at their grandparents in amazement.

"We didn't know you could be so...so sneaky!" Julia said with wide eyes. Everyone burst out laughing.

"We know how much you like treasure hunts, and we thought this would be a fun way to invite you to come to Mass with us tomorrow," said Nana. "Even though we go every week, sometimes we all could use a reminder of what a treasure Mass is."

"We had so much fun solving the mystery!" said Julia. "There's one thing I still don't understand, though. What about that line, *Where heaven touches earth*? What does it mean?"

Her grandfather lifted her into his arms. "That, my dear, is the best-kept secret of all! Every time we go to Mass, we experience the worship of heaven. Every time we go to Mass, we take part in the eternal banquet of God. So, the place where heaven touches earth...is right in your church."

"Wow!" said Peter. "I never knew that before! So, tomorrow, on the day of the sun, we get to go with you to a banquet in heaven?"

His grandmother reached out and stroked Peter's cheek. "Yes, love. Tomorrow, we get to go together to the eternal banquet, in the place where heaven touches earth. Tomorrow, we get to go to the supper of the Lamb. Tomorrow, we get to go to Mass."

"I can't wait to tell Mom and Dad when they get home," said Julia, leaning her head on her grandfather's shoulder.

"In the meantime," said James, "we have a job to do." He rolled up the scroll, tied the ribbon around it, and put it back in the box. Then he placed the invitation on top.

"Now," James said, "let's think. Whose doorstep can we leave this on next?"

Peter and Julia beamed at their older brother.

"This," said Peter, "is going to be fun."

A Note to Readers

Have you ever heard of the Book of Revelation? It is the very last book in the Bible.

In some ways, the Book of Revelation is like the scroll that Peter, Julia, and James work to decode. At first glance, the scroll seems confusing. But after the children connect the words and symbols on the scroll with the Mass, it all makes more sense. In the same way, the Book of Revelation can seem confusing at first glance, because its words and symbols are mysterious. But when we connect the words and symbols with the Mass, the Book of Revelation starts to makes more sense! There are "clues" and "hints" in the Book of Revelation that highlight the elements of the Mass.

There is even a scroll in the Book of Revelation that can only be opened by Jesus, the Lamb of God—just as the message of the scroll in this book can only be unlocked through the Mass, the supper of the Lamb.

Here are some verses that show how the things that Peter, Julia, and James discovered in the seven clues on the scroll are also found in the Book of Revelation!

FROM THE BOOK OF REVELATION

1 *The Sign of the Cross:* "[The servants of God and of the Lamb] shall worship him; they shall see his face, and his name shall be on their foreheads." (Rev 22:3–4)

2 *The priest:* "[I saw] one like a son of man, clothed with a long robe..." (Rev 1:13)

3 *Asking mercy from God, who has no beginning and no end:* "Remember then from what you have fallen, repent..." (Rev 2:5); "Holy, holy, holy is the Lord God Almighty, who was and is and is to come!" (Rev 4:8)

 4 *The Bible readings:* "Blessed is he who reads aloud the words of the prophecy, and blessed are those who hear, and who keep what is written therein..." (Rev 1:3)

 5 *The angels:* "And another angel came and stood at the altar with a golden censer; and he was given much incense to mingle with the prayers of all the saints upon the golden altar before the throne; and the smoke of the incense rose with the prayers of the saints from the hand of the angel before God." (Rev 8:3–4)

 6 *The Lamb:* "Blessed are those who are invited to the marriage supper of the Lamb." (Rev 19:9)

The Eucharist: "He who has an ear, let him hear what the Spirit says to the churches. To him who conquers I will give some of the hidden manna..." (Rev 2:17)

A Special Number

After God created the world in six days, He set aside the seventh day of the week for worship and rest. He declared the seventh day holy. After that, the number seven stood for perfection and holiness for the people of Israel. So, when you hear or see the number seven in the Bible, it is often a symbol that means something is perfect and holy!

Text copyright © 2022 Scott Hahn and Maura Roan McKeegan
Illustrations copyright © 2022 Loyola Press
Illustrations by Mercè Tous

ISBN: 978-0-8294-5515-1
Library of Congress Control Number: 2022938097
To purchase this book in bulk quantities, contact Customer Service at
800-621-1008 for information and discounts.

Printed in the United States of America.
22 23 24 25 26 27 28 29 30 31 32 CGC 10 9 8 7 6 5 4 3 2 1

LOYOLAPRESS.
A JESUIT MINISTRY

www.loyolapress.com